The Circus Surprise

by Ralph Fletcher ★ illustrated by Vladimir Vagin

Clarion Books ★ New York

Clarion Books
a Houghton Mifflin Company imprint
215 Park Avenue South, New York, NY 10003

www.houghtonmifflinbooks.com

Printed in Singapore.

Library of Congress Cataloging-in-Publication Data

Fletcher, Ralph J.
The circus surprise / by Ralph Fletcher ; illustrated by Vladimir Vagin.
p. cm.
Summary: When he gets lost at the circus, Nick is helped by a clown on stilts,
who shows him the whole circus and helps him find his parents.
ISBN 0-395-98029-1
[1. Lost children—Fiction. 2. Circus—Fiction.]
I. Vagin, Vladimir Vasil'evich, 1937– ill. II. Title.

PZ7.F632115 Ci 2001
[E]—dc21   00-057034

TWP   10 9 8 7 6 5 4 3 2 1

This book is for Santiago with all my love—R.F.

To dear brothers Jamie and Luke Buss— V.V.

Every year Mom and Dad surprised Nick on his birthday. Last year they took him to a professional basketball game and Nick got to sit on the bench with the players. The year before that they all went to a rodeo. He wondered what this year's surprise would be.

"We're taking you to the circus!" Mom told him.

"Yesssssss!" Nick said. He clapped his hands and leaped into the air. The circus!

Nick had never been to the circus before, and he didn't
want to miss a single thing. There were sword swallowers
and trapeze artists . . .

Men with huge muscles and terrifying tattoos . . .

Clowns with enormous feet and monkeys wearing funny clothes . . .

Cages with lions and cages with trained elephants. And cotton candy!

Nick followed his nose and pushed through the crowd of people until he got close to the cotton candy machine. A woman took a paper cone and swirled it around and around the inside of the machine. Soon she had a big sugary mass of blue fluff. Nick's stomach growled. His mouth began to water.

"Dad, will you buy me one?" he asked, looking up.

But instead of Dad, a stranger looked down at Nick.

"Oh, no!" Nick cried.

His heart started beating hard. He tried to remember what Dad and Mom had told him to do if he ever got lost.

1. Ask someone you can trust (like a policeman) for help.

2. Stay in one place. Don't run off.

3. Don't panic!

But Nick panicked. He ran every which way trying to find Mom and Dad. The more he ran, the more lost he got.

Finally he stopped at the lion cage. The lions stared at him, licking their lips. Nick couldn't help himself. He started crying.

"Hey, there!" a voice boomed out from way up high. "Are you lost?"

Nick looked up and saw a clown on tall stilts. The clown had a green face.

"I can't find my mom and dad." Nick wiped his eyes.

"Hey, don't worry," the clown said. "I've helped hundreds of kids find their parents. Thousands. But hey, I'll need your help. What's your name?"

"Nick."

"Nick," the clown said. "Can you climb the ladder on the back of that cage?"

"I don't know," Nick said. "It's pretty high."

"You can do it," the clown told him. "If you can make it to the top of the ladder, I'll do the rest."

"Well, OK," Nick said. He started climbing.

"Here we go!"
the clown said. He
reached over and
lifted Nick up, up, up.
The clown slid Nick
into a snug little
pouch on his back.
Nick grabbed the
clown's shoulders
and looked down.

"I'm going to fall!"
he cried.

"No, you won't,"
the clown told him.

"I've been walking on
stilts for twenty years.
You're perfectly safe
with me."

Nick couldn't believe how high up he was. He shut his eyes so he wouldn't have to look down.

"ATTENTION, PLEASE!" the clown yelled through his megaphone. "I'VE GOT A BOY WHO IS WORRIED ABOUT HIS LOST PARENTS!"

Nick thought that was funny. His parents weren't lost. He was.

"Hey, Nick!" the clown said. "Look at those kittens over there!"

Nick opened his eyes a crack. The clown was pointing at the lion cage.

"Those aren't kittens," Nick said. "Those are lions!"

"They sure look like kittens from up here," the clown said. "They look hungry, too. Somebody better give those kittens a big bowl of milk!"

Nick smiled.

"Look!" the clown said. "I see a spider hanging from a web! And I don't like spiders!"

This time the clown pointed at a monkey dangling from a rope.

"That's not a spider!" Nick said. "That's a little monkey!"

"It looks like a creepy crawly spider!" the clown said. "Let's get out of here!"

Nick giggled.

The clown started walking on his long legs. Nick held on tight. He felt dizzy being so far off the ground.

"Will you look at all those ants!" the clown said, pointing.

"Those aren't ants," Nick said. "They're people!"

"They sure look like ants from up here," the clown said. "If my pet anteater was here, he'd slurp them all up! And then he'd burp! That's all he does, slurp and burp, burp and slurp!"

This time Nick laughed.

They walked near a man who was holding a fiery torch.
The man lifted the flaming torch to his head. Then he opened
his mouth and swallowed the fire! The crowd cheered wildly.

"Wow!" Nick said. It was fun being so high up in the air.
He had a great view of everything.

Then he remembered about being lost. "But what if I never see my mom and dad again?"

"Hey, we'll find them," the clown said. "ATTENTION! ATTENTION, PLEASE! I HAVE A BOY NAMED NICK WHO IS EXTREMELY WORRIED ABOUT HIS LOST PARENTS!"

"You and I make a terrific team," the clown said. "Would you like to join the circus? I could teach you how to walk on stilts."

Before Nick could answer, he saw two people pushing through the crowd.

"That's them!" Nick cried. "MOM! DAD!"

"Nick!" Dad and Mom cried.

"Hooray!" the clown shouted. He took Nick over to the same ladder he had used before. Nick climbed out of the little backpack and down the ladder until he was folded into a double hug between Mom and Dad.

"You are a sight for sore eyes," Dad said.

Mom kissed him ten times. She smiled at the clown.

The clown smiled back. "Hey, Nick, you sure you don't want to join the circus?"

Nick looked at Dad and Mom.

"Maybe when I'm older," he said.

"OK." The clown winked. "Hey, watch your parents so they don't get lost again. Bye, Nick!"

"Bye!" He waved and watched the clown walk away on his stilts.

"I'm hungry," Nick said. "Can I get some cotton candy?"

"OK," Mom said with a smile.

"Can I get the extra-jumbo size?"

"Sure thing," Dad said. "But we have to hurry or we'll miss the show."

As they hurried to the cotton candy machine, Nick held Mom's hand, and Dad's, too.

"Were you scared?" Mom asked.

"Nope," Nick said. He thought for a moment. "Well, a tiny bit."

"How did it feel being so high up?" Dad asked.

"It was cool!" Nick told him. "I felt like the tallest basketball player in the whole wide world!"